TOP DRAFT PICK

by

LaTasha Woods

Copyright © 2021 - All Rights Reserved

This is a work of fiction. Unless otherwise indicated, all the names, characters, businesses, places, events, and incidents in this book are either the product of the author's imagination or used in a fictitious manner. Any resemblance to actual persons, living or dead, or actual events is purely coincidental.

- From a Declaration of Principles which was accepted and approved equally by a Committee of the American Bar Association and a Committee of Publishers and Associations.

In no way is it legal to reproduce, duplicate, or transmit any part of this document in either electronic means or in printed format. Recording of this publication is strictly prohibited and any storage of this document is not allowed unless with written permission from the publisher. All rights reserved.

GOLD CROWN PUBLISHING

TABLE OF CONTENTS

Chapter One 5

Chapter Two 13

Chapter Three 24

Chapter Four 35

Chapter Five 42

Chapter Six 48

Chapter Seven 61

Chapter Eight 72

CHAPTER ONE

"Click-click, click-click," the sound of red bottoms colliding with marbled floor echoed in the empty hallway. The expensive marble equally matched the expensive shoes, now beating mercilessly upon it. The lady walked down the hallway, passing through opened doors, greeting everyone, and down to the door that had the inscription, "Miss Payton Lewis". The name was engraved in gold. It was the kind you could find in one of those exquisite hotels fit for only top dignitaries of countries. The distance between the door and the chair was enough to build a racetrack, but the young lady walked confidently like she was used to standing before Kings, and like she owned the building. Of course, she owned the building, like every Payton Enterprise that existed in New York.

She had just gotten off the phone with her best friend, Avery. The young lady had tried desperately to help put her mood in a better place than it was, and it had worked partially. With a huge sigh, Payton dropped to the huge chair behind the large table, relishing in the comfort that her feet desperately needed. She had asked her assistant to clear her schedule for the night and fix her appointments for later. She adored her assistant because she always knew the right things to do, and at what time to do them.

She'd found peace in the Lord a long time ago. Her mom forced her to tag along each time she went to the local Baptist Church in their small Texas town, on days when her father wasn't coaching her to take over the world. She had experienced Jesus way before her relationship with Emory went south, long before she'd met him, and back when she'd made her first million.

As Payton let her fingers squeeze her keys, she forced her feet to rise, and resumed her poised demeanor. The trip to her house was a short one because it was a high rise. Like the expensive setting of her office, her penthouse apartment screamed wealthy. She usually liked to stay in her main apartment during the weekend. Today, she needed to remain close to town because she had a date.

An organized lady, she took off her item of clothing one at a time and calmly, neatly leaving the dirty clothes for her cleaning lady to attend to. She strolled into the adjourning room and prepared the tub for her bath. She was resolved to enjoy the rest of the evening and not let the nagging sign of impending doom spoil the fun she could get tonight. Apart from rare occasions when she had to get away from the gossips surrounding her past, she barely had enough time to register her life away from work. Payton stayed in the tub until she could feel the water go cold, and then she began her preparation to looking her best.

Payton's date, Shelton, had offered to pick her up at her residence but Payton liked to hold the power of leaving her destination without a glitch in case anything went wrong. She'd been on a lot of dates to know that she didn't like to be at the mercy of a stranger. Hence, as she parked her Range Rover at the valet of the "Royal Circle," restaurant, she wasn't surprised to not find her date already there. She let her black stilettos walk her to the center of the room where the dim light reflected brighter. From the corner of her eyes, she could see a young couple bite from a delicious-looking entree on their table, and she felt her stomach grumble in protest. The waiter walked towards her, no doubt to make an order, but Payton knew it was rude to order food before your date arrived.

"Welcome to the Royal Circle, what can I get you?" The young man said, bowing his head and placing his right arm on his chest as his upper body went down.

"I'll take water and a glass of red wine please," she responded.

Her table faced the entrance of the door and the small gold wristwatch on her left wrist sent a clear message. The date was starting almost an hour late. Shelton's neatly trimmed bearded face was nowhere in sight, and even when she thought she heard his shrill laughter more than once, the seat across hers remained empty. Payton didn't want to be rude, but she was hungry and couldn't wait any longer and had to place an order. Her taste buds savored every bite of pepper pot soup that hit her tongue and she could feel the rich ingredients in each bite. Being a good cook herself, she acknowledged the time and skills the restaurant's chefs must have put into the meal.

By the time she cleared her plate and finished the second glass of wine that she'd ordered, she knew Shelton was not going to turn up at the restaurant. She'd met him at the mall, on the same aisle, getting canned soup about a week ago and they'd both had a chat at the coffee shop not far from the mall. There had been something about how honest he was when he directly approached her. This made her say yes to the date. She could tell that the laugh lines at the corner of his eyes contrasted his fake loud laughter. She had gone out with guys like him before, who would walk into the church and search for the lady who screamed the most resounding "Amen," and hoped to sweep them off their feet. She could read his lines loud and clear. Her gut told her to stay clear. The ladies had asked her to give it a trial run, and here she was sitting next to an empty chair. Payton called for her check and settled her bill before driving home.

Payton saw the warning sign her car flashed. This reminded her that she would have to stop for gas sooner than later. She had been so occupied with her date that she hadn't filled up her tank on her way. Luckily for her, the next gas station was just around the corner, and she drove in to get her tank filled. She was shuffling through her purse for her credit card when she heard it; the shrill laughter, the same one she thought she'd heard in the restaurant. This time, she was certain about it because it was soon accompanied by his deep voice.

"I see you get your sassiness from your mother."

Payton could not resist the urge to take a backward glance and confirm her suspicion, even when she knew she'd get hurt if she did. The dip on their chin was exactly on the same spot, but the boy had the same white skin as the lady at Shelton's side. Payton watched the trio argue about something she had no idea of, and Shelton planted a quick kiss on the lips of the woman.

When Payton was little, she battled the ability to handle any kind of shock. Sometimes she'd cry, and other times, she'd lose consciousness. The event unfolding before her felt like déjà-vu, and over the years, she had learned to toughen up by taking calm slow breaths. In that same manner, Payton squared her shoulders as she completed her purchase, settled her bills, and prepared to zoom off.

"It is all for the best. He was never meant to stay anyway. He lied to you. The Lord knows best." She repeated this, as she continued the 10 minutes-drive to her penthouse.

CHAPTER TWO

"I told you to meet me at the cabin. Remind me again why I have to come to the ...?"

Payton cut off Avery's whining voice as she spoke into the receiver. Payton was behind the wheel, her hair let down, and sunglasses on the bridge of her nose. She couldn't mask the smile on her lips as she listened to her best friend's argument with the person on the line. She loved her friends, and she was glad to have them in her life. They had been friends since high school, and there was nothing that could ever break their bond. Even when they all began to settle down one way or the other, they kept their bond still tight.

The car breezed through the streets of Texas, the natural light shining brightly on them as traffic seemed to be taking a break. It was good to be home, and Payton couldn't help but glance at the small mall and lounge that she co-owned right here in her place of birth. She loved the signature of her brand name on all her businesses because it was chosen by someone special. She remembered vividly that night when Emory had helped her pick this design. He had carefully analyzed why he liked that one, and how it reminded him of her finely sculptured frame. That night, they'd made love by the fireside, two souls uniting to become one. They made a lasting memory, calling their unborn child, Carter.

"Girl, don't go getting sad on this ride. Shelton never deserved you. You ain't gon be in a slump over that piece of no good," Avery snapped her fingers in front of Payton, no doubt trying to bring her back to present times. Payton watched her natural curls bounce as she moved. She hadn't realized that she'd zoned out while driving and replaced her smile with a gloomy expression.

Two weeks ago, when Shelton stood her up on their date, Payton had gone home without calling her friends. She didn't want anyone feeling sorry for another failed attempt to revive her love life. Instead, she had gone on her knees and thanked God for preventing another major heartbreak that was bound to have happened, and then she went to bed. At 38, she refused to get tired of repeating the process of meeting someone new.

Payton caught sight of a young woman with long braids, standing in front of a one-story building just ahead. The woman was with a man holding a boy of about six years of age. Jazmine was Payton's other friend, and her husband was Payton's business partner. Both Payton and Drake, co-owned the mall that they had driven past. Drake was the original owner of the business and was rendered helpless when the business almost folded up due to mismanagement of funds. Rather than let Drake suffer in the hands of loan sharks, Payton had come to the rescue, helping make the business stand on its feet again. Payton stopped the car across the house and turned to Avery

"Look. I know you think I'm not over Shelton or Emory, and, whatever...the point is I am over all that. It's our weekend together, let's have fun and do away with work and the man drama. For Christ's sake, I need to feel a good vibe. I am home."

Her friends had suggested that they bond again, and she was past shuffling her long-needed vacation because of work; hence, she'd asked for a week to get everything tidied up and ready for her short weekend of hanging with the girls. She should take the opportunity and see her dad, but she didn't think she had it in her to listen to her father nag about her life.

"That's my baby girl. Now get that cute self of yours out the car before Jazmine begins to wonder what the holdup is about in here," Avery said.

The small boy had run towards Payton hugging her legs the moment she got out of the car with chants of "TT Payton," slicing through the air.

"Hey there big champ, how are you doing today?"

Payton saw Avery storm towards Jazmine, intending to give her a piece of her mind. She had asked the other woman to meet up with the rest of the crew at the cabin. Jazmine had made them travel into town and take a longer route on their journey.

"I'm okay. Mom says she won't be home all week and that she'd be with you," Samson said wile pouting.

"Come on baby. Do not bother TT Payton with so many questions. Come here," Jazmine said, picking up her mini-me. She kissed his one-sided dimple once, then twice before handing him to his father. Payton watched the little drama with admiration and longing. She was getting old, but she believed she'd have her baby someday.

"Payton..."

Drake's outstretched hand pointed towards Payton. He was always the one with all the formalities, but deep down, Payton knew he adored his wife and took his business seriously. She had only seen him fall apart once since she'd known him seven years ago. They had all thought their friend was crazy trying to be with a grumpy sad person.

With time, they'd realized he was vulnerable. When he'd almost lost his business, Payton could do the only thing humanly possible.

"Drake..." Payton replied taking the hand Drake offered.

"I hear you ladies are planning a coup against us men," Drake said, tickling Samson. Payton saw the joy in this family, and she was happy her friend had this precious gift.

"Not really. We only have plans to rule the world, not men," Payton said. Soon the group of friends and partners were laughing so loud, the neighbors could hear.

"Alright baby, we have to go before dark and all the monsters come out," Jazmine said to Samson, making a bad image of a walking monster. Samson seemed to enjoy the joke because he was soon laughing. It took all but five minutes to say the goodbyes and get Jazmine's small luggage in the car before they took off. The ladies sang out loud to New Edition's *Candy Girl,* as they drove away.

The journey was a one-hour trip. Soon, the car was stopping for the final time in front of their accommodations for the weekend. The cabin was normal, with each mahogany wood finely polished. They had been here before when they were still in high school. The cabin belonged to Daija's parents, the final person completing the circle of sister friends. When her father died, he'd left her with the inheritance. Payton loved this place because of the small lake behind the house, and the peace the house brings.

"Hey ladies!"

Daija emerged, just as the ladies were bringing out the boxes from the car.

"Welcome aboard my plane people," she said.

"Quit being lazy. Come help lift these big as hell bags outta this car." Avery said.

Payton realized how much she had missed the ladies. They were all unique in their way, each making the circle of friends a special unit. Years ago, when she needed a shoulder to lean on, her friends provided more than an arm and she had always prayed to God that they have genuine peace. The kind of peace that only God gives.

"You and Grey sure do look after this place very well," Avery said, stuffing some fries in her mouth. Avery's husband was white, and they'd both decided not to have children for the past couple of years that they had been together. She licked each finger clean before diving towards the perfectly grilled chicken.

"Yeah, I guess so. He's actually out of town though, and this renovation happened without him," she said passing the bottle of ketchup to Payton.

"Well, I like it... y'all ladies have lots of fun ahead of you, and I've got the perfect lineup of events," Avery said while wiping her greasy hands on a napkin. Daija was thoughtful enough to set up her Thanksgiving-themed welcome meal outside the house, with the dining overlooking the lake.

It was a beautiful sight to see. Payton thought that maybe God was in the mood for showing off, when he designed the beautiful blue and purple petals that adorned the small garden at the side of the lake. She liked how the sun reflects on the water, the rays leaving a magical glow to the ordinary water, like glitters on the little tiara that adorned her head on that faithful day when she exchanged vows with Emory.

"Tomorrow, we go hiking!" Avery announced in her signature way. She had asked that she took charge of the activities for the weekend, of course, because she had been the one to suggest that they all took a break from work.

"Don't go telling me that you can't take a break from work Payton when you are your boss. Even the Lord rested on the 7th day, so take heed woman!" She had said the moment Payton begin to protest.

Honestly, Payton just wanted to be with her friends. She missed the companionship that comes with having someone close to talk to every day. She missed the hugs and kisses from a partner, a man to plan a future with. Her divorce from Emory was a peaceful one. Although she had tried to save the marriage, Emory wasn't having it, and they both knew it was time for goodbye.

CHAPTER THREE

The humid air chilled the usually hot soil and it seemed like the habitants of the ground enjoyed the cool of the early morning. Payton adjusted the strap on her shoulder before securing her hair in a messy bun. Her outfit had been carefully picked in preparation for the long trail that her friends had decided to torture her with. She would kill to return to the comfort of her bed. She couldn't fathom why she had to be up so early if she was supposed to be on a vacation. With a heavy sigh, she adjusted the glasses on her head, before bending to check if her boots were well laced. She missed being in shoes this comfortable and her feet rejoiced for the sweet freedom from her killer heels. Payton tried to keep her composure and not laugh, as she watched Avery battle with a sheet in her hands.

"How do y'all read these lines and stuff," she said frowning.

Avery was smart as hell, but she would rather not involve herself in geography. Her specialty was medicine. Still, she championed the course of the vacation like she knew every detail.

"You know, it would help if you placed the map right and stop turning it in every direction," Jazmine joked, walking towards the confused tour guard.

"You know what? Let's just go. Nobody uses the damn maps anyway. It's not like we're in some old pirate's ship ready to hit a tempest if we took the wrong turn." Daija shrugged her slender shoulders. At 35, she looked to be in her mid-twenties, all thanks to her Godmother's blessings. She was the youngest of them all, but often, she was the most mature one and voice of reason when it became necessary.

They walked through the paths into the woods, with small bags of supplies strapped to their back.

They had been walking for a couple of hours, but each woman appeared to be more determined than ever to put in more steps. The group carried on silently. They took a break from the minute-by-minute conversation, in the first hour of their walk. It was a comfortable silence and welcomed even; the kind that accompanied a meditation. Payton wondered what each woman was considering, perhaps their jobs, husbands, and kids. Her marriage with Emory had lasted a decade, but she didn't have any children. It wasn't because she didn't conceive but after three miscarriages, she had become weary. She believed in love. Love would call her name, and she'd answer loud and clear.

She began the search for love a couple of years after finalizing her divorce with Emory, long after Emory had remarried his ghetto love. Maybe he got to know her on one of their business trips to Jamaica in the last days of their union, because he'd gotten married to her two months after their divorce. She tried to shake off the thought of infidelity from Emory, even when he started getting cold and distant in their marriage. When he had looked her over on the hospital bed like it was a normal routine to lose an unborn child, she tried to not let the words that he had spoken hurt her.

"It's fine. You'll get over this, like the others."

That was the last time he had said something lengthy to her. From there, he started to treat her like a roommate, living a routine. It wasn't a surprise when he dropped the divorce papers on the kitchen island, already signed with a note, "please sign where necessary," stuck to its side.

Payton looked around her and realized that everyone had stopped walking. They were at an open clearing, and she hadn't realized when they unanimously decided to camp here for a few hours. Each lady opened their backpacks and brought out different items, ready to have a picnic. The sun had come out in all its glory and Payton confirmed that the time was just 11 a.m. The small basket Jazmine carried was quickly emptied on a small blanket in the center. The women had been up early to make a variety of baked goodies, drinks, and snacks.

"It feels good to breathe," Jazmine said, biting into some pancakes.

She cleaned the corner of her lips and worked her way to another bite of the almost cold food. She had tamed her mass of hair in a single braid at the back of her head.

"Yeah, I miss this, and I miss us," Daija agreed, casually sipping a liquid that Payton knew was orange juice.

Payton knew she had to at least say something, even if she wasn't up to it. She had to say something outside of business and making a ton of money with nobody to share with. She had a handful of charity donations going on in her life, and she'd also had thoughts of adopting a baby once or twice before, but she didn't want to parent her child alone. Hence, she was patiently waiting on God for her rightly ordained partner.

"How have you guys been really?" Payton said, settling for a neutral topic.

"Drake keeps pushing for another one," Jazmine revealed as she tried hard to act nonchalant.

"Well, that's great right?" Avery said, holding Jazmine's shaky hands.

"I don't want another one Avery, at least not now," she said. The tears of evidence showed in her eyes.

"Have you discussed this with him?" Avery questioned.

"No. He seems so enthusiastic about it, and I don't want to let him down," Jazmine responded.

"Jazmine, you have to tell him and find out his thoughts on waiting some more. Don't you think so?" Payton offered her friend who was sniffing away light tears.

"I don't know how to do this, and I don't want to hurt him."

"He is your husband. You'll hurt yourself if you keep bearing this burden alone, and it might lead to something worse." Payton replied, remembering how she watched Emory go distant over the years, letting a solvable issue escalate and wreck her marriage.

"I know. I'm thinking of talking to him about it. It's just that I need the right time to set things straight between us," Jazmine sniffed, grabbing a tissue from Avery whose arm was around her.

"I'm sorry for nagging. How are you, Payton?"

Jazmine said swiftly diverting the attention of the group to Payton.

Payton felt like discussing your heartfelt issue should never be considered nagging, but she let it slide as three pair of eyes turned toward her, waiting for an answer. She wished her friends realized that she was okay and that they stopped looking at her with pity. They had been there during the divorce, and they all comforted her when she cried for what she knew was the best decision to take. They had also been there when she went on the first postdivorce date. Of course, they set her up for that meet and greet many months ago. Travis was a nice man, and they had something for a couple of months until she found out he was only after her money. An unexpected visit to his home revealed that she was a backup plan for his failing business. In fact, they had not accidentally bumped into each other during one of her night runs; it had all been part of his plan.

The girls were also there when Nelson tried to convince her from going to church because he didn't believe in "her God", or when Justin stood her up on her date, all within a three-year time frame. Still, she wasn't as dejected as they expected her to be, and she knew why.

"I'm fine. Not perfect, but fine. I'm grateful for the things I have, and those yet to come. I'm grateful for my family, my beautiful friends, and this weekend away from work. I'm grateful for Jesus, for the air, water..." she smiled.

"What are you thankful for?" She asked, looking each one in the eye.

"I'm thankful for my family, food, life, my beautiful friends..." Daija began.

"Well I'm grateful for my family, my job, provision, life, and you," Avery said, bashfully smiling.

"I'm grateful for my son, my husband, my beautiful friends, and everything" Jazmine rounded up.

They all had something to be grateful for. As they sat in silence looking at each other Payton thought she heard something in the woods. The ladies must have heard it too because they all turned toward the same direction.

"I don't want to gooooooo..." a small whining voice yelled breathlessly. Payton put out her hand to stop the kid from colliding with the picnic basket, as he ran top speed.

Each woman rose to their feet in attack mode, looking around and waiting for the child's pursuer as they tried to shield the child from danger. Then they heard it. It was the heavy thud of boots. Payton said a silent prayer and with little time to prepare, grabbed her pocketknife.

CHAPTER FOUR

"I wanna hike some more, I don't wanna go..." The small boy pouted behind Payton. He looked to be around the age of five. A man emerged from the woods hot on his heels. The man looked pissed off. The striking resemblance was non-negotiable, but the man's face had a sharper angle, contrasting the round face of the boy.

"Get back here Devin, we're going home now. I'm sorry ladies, my son seems to like the hike way too much," the man said, his eyes never leaving the boy's presence.

Payton had heard of stories where children became victims to kidnapping and abuse through this same tactic, and she didn't want to take chances. She stooped at eye level with the kid. He had cute brown eyes. She held his small hands and spoke to him gently.

"My name's Payton. What's your name?"

"My name's Devin. My dad calls me Dee. I wanna hike so 'more," Devin said.

"Is that your dad over there?" Payton pushed.

Dee nodded, with cute lashes fanning his eyes. A glance the other way, showed that the poor man was getting frustrated with the whole issue.

"Do you want to go home with your dad?" She inquired.

"Yes. I want to stay longer. Pretty please dad," Dee pleaded, looking at his father for the first time since he ran to their spot. Almost immediately, his father's angry face seemed to melt. Payton saw the unrefined bond between father and son, and she knew the other women could feel it too. She looked at Avery who was watching with a wide grin on her face, and Jazmine who was gathering the cutlery. Daija was wrapping up the blankets, as she prepared for the trip back to the cabin.

"I've got to take you home to Nora, you know this..."Devin's father began to say.

"Alright Dee, why don't you go home with daddy and the next time you go hiking, I'll make sure daddy stays a little longer" Payton lied.

"Really?" Devin's face lit up at once.

"Yeah. Only if you go home with daddy." Payton rose to her feet, her knees already hurting from squatting for so long.

"I will, I will. Let's go, Daddy. Come on, come on," Devin raced to his father already eager to go home.

Payton took the moment to properly take in the duo. Devin's father had lifted his child on arms on hands that looked strong enough to crush the kid if he wanted. He was wearing a black sweater and had rolled the sleeves to reveal forearms roped with just the right amount of vein. His salt and pepper beard was the only hair visible on his face, and his head was bald.

"Of course we will, but not without saying goodbye to Payton and her friends." The man seemed at ease now that his son was not running away from him. He'd taken a step forward, then two, stretching his free hand in greeting.

"I'm Noah, dad to this sprinter here. "His deep voice vibrated, shaking each hand that was offered alongside names.

When he got to her, she placed her small hands in his, letting it swaddle her fingers. Rather than feeling threatened, the hand was warm, soft, and gentle, lingering for a second too long as she tried to think of what to say.

"My name's Payton." This was something he had already learned but she couldn't focus so her thoughts and words were everywhere.

"Thank you," the deep voice resonated.

His eyes were a darker shade complimenting, his deep voice. As they held Payton's brown-colored ones, it looked like he was searching for something deep, way deeper than the surface could offer.

"Dad, come on," Devin's tiny voice pulled them both from a daytime trance, a jolt to reality.

The goodbyes became hurried from here, each one preparing for the life ahead of them. The walk back to the cabin was shorter than the hike to the site where they held their picnic. Payton felt that it was because of the stories of Samson's mischievous act, just like the stunt Devin played. Payton could not help but wonder who and where his mother was. Now, Jazmine was narrating how Samson nearly got his father arrested when he attempted to feed some chocolates to a gorilla at the zoo.

The ladies laughed till their stomachs hurt, and by the time they reached the cabin, the sun was just setting. Payton quickly took off her hiking gear and opened the backdoor that would lead her to the lake path. The reflection of the setting sun was already on the waters, and she brought out her iPhone to take a picture. She'd add it to the million copies of nature she was collecting when she got back home. For now, she let her eyes savor the beauty before her.

"This is such a beautiful scenery. I don't think I can ever get tired of watching one of God's many wonders right at my doorstep," Daija said. She joined Payton on the soft grass where she had made herself comfortable. The water was more beautiful from this spot, and you could watch the birds in their natural habitat without disturbing them.

"Nature soothes the body and soul. It is always an antidote to a troubled mind. When I was younger, my dad would bring me out to the cabin, and let us sit at this exact spot, watching the sunset, until its beautiful golden color disappeared." Payton had no words to offer so she sat silently enjoying the view.

CHAPTER FIVE

Monday marked the start of new beginnings. For Payton, it meant going back to her life of being CEO of Payton Enterprise. Payton killed the engine of her favorite black Range Rover and checked that her briefcase contained all that it was supposed to hold, before handing her keys to her assistant. Today, she was coming into the office from her home.

"I hope you enjoyed your weekend Ann," Payton asked the young lady as she adjusted her reading glasses in anticipation of her schedule for the day. Payton had an idea of about half of her schedule, but she often likes her assistant to go through it in the morning before she set in.

"Very well Payton. I hope you did too," Ann replied politely. She took the seat across from her boss.

"Alright, let's have it," Payton grabbed her sticky notes and pen, ready to get the day running.

"There is a rescheduled meeting slated between you and the bankers by 10, a noon conference with the board from the insurance company, and a 1 o'clock meeting between you and the representatives of Lorenzo d'Alberto," Ann said, placing her tablet on the table.

"Okay, thanks. I'll be working late and might need to have an early lunch. Please send in my usual, immediately after the 1 o'clock," Payton said, already settling into work.

The day crawled on slow as heck, and the meetings seemed to take forever to get rounded off. Many times, she had to ask a speaker to repeat certain points, as her mind kept drifting toward a certain bald man. She had given herself the stern talk this morning in the bathroom. She reminded herself that he was married, and it was a sin to interfere in other people's marriages. Since she herself was a divorcee, she didn't want to be the cause of another wrecked home. She had to admit that she couldn't keep her thoughts from revolving around Noah.

She checked her Apple watch and realized that she had less than five minutes until her 1 o'clock. There was no time to squeeze in lunch. Even while her stomach protested her lack of food since morning, she was determined to start the meeting on time.

The team of gentlemen who walked in, ran a construction company that had successfully laid the foundation for many top buildings in the city. They had come to discuss a new structure for Payton and Drake's business in Texas. Drake had recommended this company for the job. He had called to say that he wouldn't be able to fly in, and had instead, asked Payton to handle discussions before leaving it to the committee in charge.

Payton must have been deliriously exhausted, because she didn't notice Noah in the room until he had called out her name. The richness in his voice quickly sparked memories of that moment in the woods, and images of a cute, dimpled boy flashed before her.

"Noah. What a pleasant surprise. Please have a seat," she offered. She couldn't believe the coincidence this was, but she tried to remain cool and collected.

Payton felt that the meeting was too short. She didn't think she could handle all of Noah in the same space anymore, especially since he was the CEO of the company. Not that she expected less of him, but she didn't think it was a bright idea to have Noah this close to her. The project would span six months. It was a major one, and huge enough to have the CEO attend the meeting himself. She caught herself not wanting to say goodbye to Noah, and instead yearning to explore the depth of his eyes, the same ones that put her under a spell about 14 days ago.

"Can I buy you lunch? My way of saying thank you for the other day," he asked as she walked him to the door.

Just then, Payton's stomach chose to betray her, letting out a loud growl. The pair laughed at the irony. Even when she knew her legs should move her in the opposite direction and run the rest of the way, her heart felt at ease. Payton couldn't explain how something so wrong could feel so right. A glance at his hands showed no signs of a wedding band, nor any markings that he'd taken them off at one point. Maybe he was divorced, just like she was.

She told herself to breathe calmly because she knew nothing about him yet.

"What do you think?" A smiling Noah asked.

"Sure. I don't mind," Payton replied. She led the way.

CHAPTER SIX

It's been two weeks since Payton had lunch with Noah, at the small restaurant across her office. Although they hadn't had enough time to discuss at length, he had told her general things about his life, and they had enjoyed each other's company. One thing Payton picked up on was that he loved his son. Sadly, she didn't come around to the point where they talked about Devin's mom, but she knew Noah was single. When he asked her out on a proper date, she couldn't resist the yes that came from her lips. Noah seemed to be a man of many surprises. He'd declined her restaurant selection and had instead, offered that they had a private meeting at the park for the evening. She was grateful to God that she didn't have to wear heels, and she'd opted for a pair of sneakers. That day, she had watched the simple things about him. How he let her walk on the left side away from the road, how he opened the doors for her and pulled out her chair for her to sit before he sat. They laughed until they cried. He'd also made sure to wait until she started her car before leaving.

"When did your car start making that sound?" He asked, with a concerned look on his face.

"Uhm, what sound?" Payton asked, looking genuinely confused.

"Can you hand me your keys for a second?" He asked, while urging her out of the car.

He'd proceeded to turn on the ignition multiple times, and then he went to his car to bring out some tools. Payton watched him touch and screw on a couple of things, before asking her to get back in.

"There you go. It's all fixed." He wiped his hands on a rag.

Their goodbye was a short one, with Payton promising to call as soon as she got home safely.

During her early morning meditation, she had asked God to give her a sign. Acts of service was her love language, and he was not lacking in action. She asked for anything to confirm she was on the right track. She felt that her curiosity to know Noah more, was gradually dragging her deeper into his world. It was for this reason; she chose to tread gently.

Tonight, Payton had laid out her favorite black dress on her king-sized bed. She was going to compliment it with a black strapless purse, and a black pair of strappy sandals. Like the other dates that she had been on, she had taken out time to glam up. Unlike the rest, she kept this one a secret from her girls. As was her tradition, she had picked the restaurant. She drove herself in her car, resisting Noah's offer to decide where they should eat countless times. As she applied the final coat of mascara, she replayed the event of the previous day.

"Would you do me the honors of going out to dinner?" He asked this, as he walked her from yet another lunch break, which was becoming a weekly routine.

"Have you not fed me enough? I just had lunch," she had replied bashfully.

Something he seemed to do out of habit; he stroked his beard trying to rephrase his question.

"I'm sorry, that came out wrong. Would you please go out on a date with me, again? Anywhere you want to go is fine," he said, placing his hands in his pocket. A casual gesture, yet he managed to make it seem so extraordinary.

This time, she chose an Italian restaurant, the one behind Mrs. Browns. This place is where she often got her favorite pastries. Knowing the place oh so well, she was quite impressed when she found that Noah had made a reservation at such short notice. As Payton let the waiter usher her to her table, she caught sight of Noah standing up in recognition.

"Hi."

"Hi back stranger," Payton said, letting Noah kiss her cheek politely.

He walked to the other side of the table and pulled out her chair, letting her sit before he returned to his side of the table.

"You look beautiful," he complimented. He focused his eyes on her face, like he was trying to memorize each detail and angle.

"Thank you. You clean up nice yourself," she said. That statement did not honestly, do enough justice to his assembling of a white button-down shirt, blue jeans, and a black blazer. He looked as handsome as he had been when he ran into the clearing in the woods as a father, and when he had walked into her office as a businessman.

Picking up the menu, he ordered the *Spaghettia Alla Carbonara*. Based on his recommendation, she did the same. Once they'd cleaned their plates, they ordered a chocolate cake, as they made small talk. Noah would be 42 in a month, and he owned Lorenzo d'Alberto, by inheritance. He also revealed that he had been married once when he was 30, but he had lost his wife, during childbirth to Devin.

"I see her each time I look at him. And even if it's been 4 years, it still hurts like it was yesterday," he said.

He hadn't been interested in starting something new because he feared that not everyone would accept Devin. Payton wondered how anyone would not like the adorable kid. The rest of dinner went on way too fast, and Payton was beginning to feel her chin hurt from too much laughing.

"When I share my divorce story, people wonder why I still let my heart open to vulnerability. I've come to realize that true love, is love in Christ. No matter what, there is no perfection in humans. We must love like he loves us," Payton said, rounding off her divorce story.

Unlike the other dates that she had been on, Noah never attempted to touch her in an offensive manner. Noah held open her car door as they prepared to say goodbyes. Standing close to him, he towered over her 5'6 frame by at least a head's difference. He made her car look small, compared to when she stood next to it. She could smell his cologne. It was something manly, mixed with the scent of his aftershave; a smell that promised to linger even after he left.

"Have a safe trip home and please call me once you get home safely," he pleaded. He waited for her affirmative,

"Yes I will. I promise."

She saw him battle with himself, as his hands twitched in his pocket, perhaps trying to restrain himself from holding her hands. He eventually said goodnight and turned toward his car. She drove slowly, reliving each moment that night, and smiling to herself like she has a schoolgirl crush. The glow on her face was not because of the reflection of the streetlights that littered the street when she headed home.

"Good evening Scott," she said to the doorman who escorted her into the building as she rode the elevator to her apartment. The ding on her phone signified that she had a message.

"I hope you're home safe. If you're not driving, please call me," the text read.

Not wanting to seem too desperate, she changed into her nighties and wiped off her makeup before placing the call.

"Hi," she said.

"Hi," the rich voice replied.

"Are you home?" He asked.

"Yeah, I just got home. You?" She said into the receiver.

"Yeah, I did. I had a great time today, thank you," Noah said.

"Thank you too," Payton replied awkwardly, not used to having this conversation after a date.

"I was wondering if you'd like to come with me to a business gathering next weekend. I could use your contribution," Noah said.

"That is if you don't mind, I mean," he quickly added, faltering at the end.

Payton felt her head swell, but she felt that she needed to set some boundaries between them before she gave him the wrong idea.

"I'd have loved to, but I'll be hanging out with the girls next weekend," she lied blatantly.

"Oh! It's cool. I'd love to hang out with you some other time, please let me know when you'll be free," he said.

The hurt from her rejection was evident in his voice.

"I'll do so, thank you. Have a good night's rest," Payton said reluctantly.

"I see you. When I look at you, I see just you," Noah said, not mincing words.

There were no words from Payton, because she didn't know how best to respond to his confessions. She remained silent, and as the minutes passed, Noah spoke again.

"Goodnight Payton," he said, and Payton heard the click.

Payton felt her insides melt, then come alive like she was 22 again. She felt like she was young and wild, and free as a bird. The last time she'd felt this way was many years ago when Emory won her heart, and even then, she didn't feel all giddy. The screen of her phone lit up, signifying an incoming message.

"I hope you dream of a garden filled with beautiful white roses. Noah."

The text carried an attachment which she opened. It was a picture of Noah looking very at ease, in a jersey.

"Whose Jersey is this?" she typed smiling at her phone. She was used to people wearing sports clothing, just for the fun of it.

"Michael Jordan. Why?" He replied.

"I'm a huge sports fan and I love basketball. Do you play?" She typed.

"No but I love to watch. I was at the last state's championship game with some friends," he typed back.

"That's awesome. I also love to watch. I played some basketball when I was in high school." "Maybe you would do me the honors of seeing a game with me sometimes," he typed.

"Okay," Payton replied.

"Goodnight Payton," Noah typed.

"Goodnight Noah," she responded for the second time that night. She felt everything was happening too fast. He is perfect. It's gotta be a catch. All this attention he was giving, even though she knew she was worth it. She had a lot to offer and loved hard. Many men were attracted to her, but they didn't value her. He knew she was a real one. She deserved this. Wasn't this what she prayed for? She sighed loudly and hoped that she'd find some time to sleep, even when Noah occupied her thoughts.

CHAPTER SEVEN

"Miss Lewis, you have a delivery," her secretary said poking her head into the room. This was the third delivery in the last three weeks. Payton wondered what surprise Noah had in store for her, this time around. The first delivery had been flowers and chocolates with a rainbow-colored card that had unicorn designs at the back of the card. She had broken down in a fit of laughter in the middle of the hallway and had earned the stare of her staff. The second one was very romantic. He'd gotten her a nice red dress and asked that she dressed up for dinner in an hour. He had gone through the trouble of sending a chauffeur to pick her up in a nice limousine. The chauffeur dropped her off at a five-star restaurant she'd never visited, and she had spent the rest of the evening at the beach with Noah. Thinking about it, Payton realized she'd broken quite a lot of rules for this man. She'd let him surprise her by picking out a restaurant and left her car at home on a date.

"Thank you, Ann. Please bring it in here," Payton said. She was thinking of how she'd break the news to Avery, who was currently sitting on her couch. Her eyes were wide, as April carried the massive variety of flowers into her office. Payton carefully, and slowly arranged the bright flowers, beside the white rose that had been delivered before.

What was she going to tell Avery? What was she doing with Noah, going on dates, sharing hugs, and having long calls with both him and his son? She was receiving gifts and being spoiled for the past four months.

"Hmm hmmm hmm. Someone's got a huge admirer. Don't we?" Avery began the inevitable conversation, that would soon be heard among her friends.

"Shut up. It's nothing serious. Noah's just a showoff," Payton replied, failing to hide her blush.

"Wow, I see our admirers got a name, Noah it is then. Who is this Noah?" She pressed on, like a mother questioning her child. Payton couldn't believe that her friend had forgotten such a fine specimen within just four months.

"You'll meet him soon," she said. She was grateful to God that she didn't have to hold that conversation just yet. "You bet I will, girl," she said, clapping and rising to her feet.

"Remind me why you're in my office again?" Payton spoke, back pretending to be angry.

"To ask some questions and I think I've gotten my answers. I'm telling the girls about this mystery man. I think it's time for a conference call. Tell mystery man to get ready to be sanctioned, because I'm one hundred percent sure that he's the reason why you didn't grace my housewarming ceremony." Avery said, rising to leave.

"Oh my God, that was last weekend. I'm sorry Avery, it escaped my mind," Payton explained.

"It's fine, friend. I've not seen you glow this way in a long time, and I'm happy that you're happy. You deserve all of God's favor."

Payton felt tears prickling her eyes, and she let them fall only after she had seen Avery off the door. The flowers brightened up the room. He knew her favorites were lilies and tulips. They were so many. They drove home a meaning that he knew what he wanted, and he was going to get it. A small red card that accompanied the flowers carried a handwritten text.

Dinner at my place tonight?

Xo, Noah.

Payton sank into her chair with the card in hand. She didn't know what to tell her friends about Noah, but she knew that she cared about him, and she wanted everything he had to offer.

"You sure have extreme confidence," she said into the phone.

"What can I say? Your charm brings out the confidence in me. Do you mind if my Mom joins us for dinner?" Noah replied, straight to the point.

"Uhm...I mean, if, uhm she's around, why not?" She wasn't scared of his Mother, but she didn't know if she was ready to meet her.

"Thank you, babe. You're going to love her."

Babe? Payton felt like she'd just been offered the million-dollar lottery.

"Uhm, okay," as she tried to play it off.

"I'll see you by 7. Dress comfortably," he said, and then the click sounded.

This was the part where she needed Jazmine or Daija to calm her down and help her prepare for this meet and greet. She wasn't announcing anything, until she was certain that what they had was heading somewhere. Payton checked her time and realized it was just a little past four. Still, she closed for the day and rode the elevator down to the parking garage. She had never been to Noah's house, but common sense told her she'd need to bring something along. Hell, she hadn't even asked the kind of meal he'd be preparing, and if he needed extra hands in the kitchen.

In her panic, she remembered the routine of taking steady breaths to help retain the calm, to draft out a plan. First, she'd stop by Mrs. Brown's and pick up her favorite cheesecake. She'd add a bottle of red wine and a box of chocolates for Devin.

By 6:55 pm, she was in her car, in search of Noah's house. For someone who owned a multimillion construction company, Payton didn't expect anything less than the crafty structure before her. From the gate, each angle of the single-story building seemed to be carefully detailed. She parked her next to his vehicle; the Corvette she'd seen him drive countless times. She opened her door, wondering if Noah's mother was already in the house or if she would join them later. She knew that Noah came from money but there wasn't nearly enough time to get anything fancier for his mom.

"Payton!" Devin came running from the door and out into Payton's outstretched arm. Payton was getting used to the big guys running habit.

"How are you doing darling?" she asked.

"I'm okay. Grandma's here and she made plenty of food for us. Come see!" He happily yelled, not minding the pie and other stuff Payton was trying hard to balance, as he persistent pulled.

"Dee, why don't you help Payton with her bags first," that rich sensual voice spoke, immediately lighting up the already well-lit atmosphere.

Payton stared at the handsome man in front of her, who had managed to make her breathing hitch, and she remained transfixed to the floor like one of the electric poles she'd driven past as she came here. As Noah approached, she found herself struggling to open and close her mouth like a fish on dry land, desperate for water. He walked confidently towards her and planted a firm kiss on her lips, before taking the pie from her unsteady hand.

"How are you gorgeous?" He asked, leading the way to the front steps.

"I'm good. Thank you," she replied. She forced her hair around her face, to hide the blush she could feel.

"You're right on time for dinner. My mother has been expecting you," he said. They finally reached the living room.

The house was beautifully decorated with grey, white, and black as the theme colors. The house was massive and cozy at the same time, but she was drawn to the paintings of Devin on the wall. They were four paintings of baby Devin, as he grew.

"Babe, I want you to feel at home around my family. You'll love Mom," he said, holding her hands.

He gave her hands a gentle squeeze one last time before leading the way to an area she soon found out was the dining room. Noah's mother was by no means a small woman. Instead, Payton saw a tall, slim, elegant, and agile woman with long strands of grey hair.

"Mom, meet my girlfriend, Payton. Payton, my Mom," Noah said.

Payton froze when she heard the word girlfriend. Did he say girlfriend?

"Hi, Mrs. Reed. It's a pleasure meeting you."

"The pleasure's all mine. Please call me Sharon, dear," she said. She patted her lightly on her cheek.

CHAPTER EIGHT

Ms. Sharon was an extremely nice woman, and a great cook too. She had fixed enough food to feed a small crowd. Payton admired her kind gesture, and she was forced to take home a couple of leftovers, despite her protests. That night, after Noah walked Payton to her car, he brought out two tickets from his pocket.

"There's a game coming up next weekend, and I'd like you to come with me," Noah said looking into her eyes.

Payton collected the tickets and read the details. They were tickets to watch the state's basketball game, scheduled for next week. She always attended the game. She was certain that Ann must have made a reservation, as was her tradition, but she took the tickets anyway.

"Wow. I love to watch this game. I'd love to go," Payton said. She felt that Noah's effort was so sweet. They both said their goodbyes, and he planted a firm kiss on her forehead before she drove off.

The week went by fast, perhaps because of Payton's sports date with Noah. Soon it was Saturday, and she was getting ready to have some fun. She drove herself down to the stadium and walked to the basketball arena, enjoying the cool evening breeze. Noah was nowhere in sight, and the seat numbers on the tickets were already occupied. Payton looked around the court. She was about to call Ann for her reservation details when she heard someone call out her name.

"Payton, come with me," Noah said extending his hands. She took his hands and let him lead her to the VIP courtside section.

"This is nice. I must say that I am impressed. Why did you change plans?" She asked.

"Let's say I know a guy who did me the favor. I figured you would like to be closer to the action," Noah replied.

The game commenced almost immediately, and Payton couldn't keep her eyes off an excited Noah. Sometimes she'd catch him staring at her. By the time the game ended, she could already feel the sizzling tension between them burning brighter. Noah urged her to her feet and led her towards a small glass room, away from the crowd. Here, they had a good view of what was happening outside, but the noise was minimal.

With no words said, Noah took her hand in his and moved an inch closer. She let his hands warm hers, and she squeezed his gently. When he looked into her eyes almost too long, she let herself drown in his gaze. As his face moved closer to hers and his mouth touched hers, she shut her eyes and let herself feel him. His full lips pecked her smaller ones, testing the waters and seeking permission. She knew that her approval could change things between them, and she wanted things to change between them; hence she opened her mouth and let him kiss her. At that moment it was just two of them, alone in the open. He deepened the kiss some more, angling his head to take all of her. When Noah pulled away, he framed her face with his big hands before speaking.

"From the moment I set my eyes on you, I felt a pull, a connection I couldn't deny. I liked that you talked to my child with so much love, even when you knew nothing about us. The past few months have been blissful for me. I don't know how you do it, but you light up my heart and make me want to get closer to you," he said, pausing to clear his throat.

"I want all of you and I want to give you all of me. I want you to be my queen and me, your king. I want us to build an empire together," he said holding her hands more firmly.

Payton let him caress her hands as she tried to compose her words.

"I want all of that too and I want to be by your side," she said through smiles.

"Is that a yes?" Noah asked hopefully.

"Yes," Payton nodded, giggling. Noah looked like he had just been handed a winning lottery ticket.

"Can I tell the world that we are together?" He asked.

"Yes," Payton said. She felt her heartbeat returning to normal as she looked at Noah's face. It seems like we had both been drafted and selected as the #1 pick. She couldn't wait to explore the future with Noah, and she prayed silently that they would last.

NOTES

Made in the USA
Columbia, SC
04 September 2024